CW00847914

PERLEY the PARROT goes to PRIDE

Written by KATIE GLENN

Illustrated by ALICE BURTON HALL

Perley was awoken when the lights flicked on above,
"Well good morning Perley," said a spritely Mrs Love.
She weaved around the tables to put out paper and pens,
Before opening the door to welcome all of Perley's friends.

Little Luke threw his bag on the floor by his peg,

And Aida went flying over a stuck out chair leg.

This was all before the morning bell had rung, But that was all normal for the children of Millsprung.

"What's wrong?" asked Mrs Love
when she saw Lily all alone.

"It's nothing really" Lily said
"I just feel so on my own."

"Jamie said I was different, because I have two dads, I didn't tell Jamie but it's made me really sad."

"Our families are all different," Mrs Love assured her.

Perley had never thought of families outside
of the room.
He'd always lived alone and thought that
children did too.
Perley felt inspired to learn more about these
things,
So he hopped up and down, closed his eyes
and began to flap his wings.

Quick as a flash, Perley was on a bright flag in the sky,
He looked around for clues and signs and read the word
'PRIDE'.

Music was booming brilliantly and there was colour all around,
He looked down below him and saw a gigantic crowd!

Amongst the crowd he saw a friendly sloth
with a beaming grin.
"I have no idea where I am," Perley cried.
"Can you please fill me in?"

"This is a Pride parade my parrot,
I'll take you round with me!"
"Pride?" Perley wondered, but he thought he'd
wait and see.

The sloth said to call them Sammie, then
talked all about the parade.
They said Pride was a celebration of love and
the progress that had been made.

"People now feel more comfortable to express
who they are inside,
This could mean dressing differently, or loving
whoever they love with pride."

"Boys can love boys, boys can love girls and girls can love girls too,
Plus, not everyone wants to be defined by the colours pink and blue."

"So why do people march like this if life is just that way?"
"Because" Sammie replied "people haven't been as nice as they are today."
"Over the years it's gotten much better but some people are still unkind."

Finally Perley understood what he'd come here to find.
Jamie hadn't meant to be mean, he just didn't understand,
Maybe there's something Perley could do to lend a helping hand...

"Mind if I take this?" Perley asked,
pointing at Sammie's flag.

"Take as many as you like Perley, there are
plenty in my bag."

Perley thanked Sammie for their help and explained he must return. He had to get back and spread the word of everything he'd learnt.

And just like that, he was
back in his cage on top
of his little log...

"What's that in Perley's cage?" Jamie let out with a cry.
"That's a mini flag I think, a little flag of PRIDE."
"What's Pride Miss?" Jamie shouted, interrupting again.
"Good question Jamie," Mrs Love replied
and answered it there and then.

She talked about identity, and all different
kinds of love,
Then Perley looked and saw Jamie give Lily
a hug.
He apologised for what he'd said, he just
did not know.
Mrs Love said mistakes are okay, we're all
learning and growing. So...

With that Perley realised that his work here
was done,
The children had learnt about differences and
that you can love anyone...

Love who you are, he thought, as he settled
down to sleep.
He was excited for what tomorrow might bring
and the new people he might meet!

Printed in Great Britain
by Amazon

83086686R00018